Tarantula Power!

by Ann Whitehead Nagda

illustrated by
Stephanie Roth

Holiday House / *New York*

For Beth Ward's fourth-grade class
and Nando Gonzalez,
librarian at Pioneer Elementary
A. W. N.

For Mrs. Jordan
and Mrs. Brade,
thank you for bringing out
the best in children
S. R.

Library of Congress Cataloging-in-Publication Data
Nagda, Ann Whitehead, 1945–
Tarantula power! / by Ann Whitehead Nagda ; illustrated by Stephanie Roth.
p. cm.
Summary: Forced to work with the class bully on a project to
design a new breakfast cereal, Richard also tries to stop him from
picking on second-graders by using tarantula power.
ISBN-13: 978-0-8234-1991-3 (hardcover)
ISBN-10: 0-8234-1991-6 (hardcover)
[1. Schools—Fiction. 2. Bullies—Fiction. 3. Cereals, Prepared—Fiction.
4. Tarantulas—Fiction.] I. Roth, Stephanie, ill. II. Title.

PZ7.N13355Tar 2007
[Fic]—dc22
2006043392

Chapter 1

Richard chewed on his lip and stared at the paper on his desk. "Invent a Cereal," the paper said.

They were supposed to be brainstorming. Richard turned his paper over and waited for a storm to develop. He drew clouds, then put his pencil down. He rolled the pencil back and forth across his desk. He picked up the pencil and drew drops falling from the clouds.

Suddenly, he had an idea. "Hailstones," he wrote, "the destructive cereal. Little globs of ice." He shook his head. Not too nourishing, unless you were lost in the desert.

"If you have an idea you're not sure about, share it with one of your classmates," said Mrs. Steele.

Richard drew a lightning bolt. "Fire Crackles, the explosive cereal. Start your day with a bang!" He pictured cereal shooting out of the bowl. Kids would love it! Well, maybe. Susan wouldn't love it. It was too messy. He wasn't sure what his teacher would think. He sighed. His ideas were so weird.

Next, he drew some fish swimming in an ocean. A shark was after them. He drew a big fin sticking out of the water. "Shark Attack!" he wrote. "Scare yourself awake in the morning." He pictured hundreds of shark fins slicing through milk. Hmm, not bad.

Richard looked around. In front of him, Jenny was bent over her paper. Next to her, Susan had set down her pen. She was always the first one finished. Kevin, who sat on Jenny's other side, had rolled his paper into a tube and was using it like a telescope. When Kevin leaned over Jenny's paper, she batted him away.

An ant crawled across Richard's paper. With one whop of his fist, he terminated the ant.

Rana, who sat next to Richard, wrinkled her nose and moved her chair, so that she was sitting as far from him as she could.

Jenny turned around. She watched as Richard flicked the ant onto Susan's flowered blouse.

"Bull's-eye!" Richard grinned at Jenny.

She grinned back, then reached over and brushed the ant off Susan's shoulder.

"What was that?" asked Susan.

"A nutritious snack," said Richard.

"Just a little bug," said Jenny. "It's gone."

Susan shivered. "Ick!"

That gave Richard another idea. He turned his paper over. "Crunchy Critters," he wrote for the name of his cereal. "Bug friends in the shape of crickets, grasshoppers, and spiders." He had to think of a good slogan. "Gives you power to crawl, climb, jump, and . . ." What else? Spin webs? No. Fly? Yes, that was better. Sort of. He turned his paper back to the stormy side.

Kevin stood beside him, his telescope trained on Richard's crazy ideas. "Wow!" said Kevin. "You have lots of cereals."

Kevin had said something nice. Richard was surprised. "Which one do you like?"

"Fire Crackles, the explosive cereal!" said Kevin. "That's awesome."

"What do you think about Shark Attack?" asked Richard.

"That's okay," said Kevin, "but Fire Crackles sounds more like a cereal name."

Kevin used his paper telescope to look at Rana's paper and then Susan's.

"Do your own work, Kevin," said Susan.

"We're supposed to help each other," Kevin whined.

"Okay," said Susan. "What's your idea?"

He thought a minute. "How about Fish Feast?"

"Fish Feast!" she said. She shook her head and her curls bounced. "That sounds like cat food."

Kevin frowned and slunk back to his desk. He sat there swinging his legs back and forth.

Richard watched Kevin drum a pencil on the desk. Kevin was always moving, like a snake looking for prey.

Richard turned his paper over and read all his cereal ideas again. He liked Shark Attack the best. He looked up at the clock. No time left.

"I can't wait to hear some of your ideas," said Mrs. Steele.

Susan's hand shot up. No surprise there.

"Yes, Susan," said Mrs. Steele.

"The name of my cereal is Flower Power. Each piece of cereal will be made in the shape of a different flower." Susan looked at Mrs. Steele and smiled. She continued, "There will be roses, daffodils, daisies, tulips, pansies, nasturtiums, chrysanthemums, and many other flowers. My slogan is, 'Start your day in a summer garden.' On the back of the package

I'll have pictures of the flowers and information about them."

"Very nice, Susan," said Mrs. Steele. "I see you've already started to design the box for your cereal."

Rana raised her hand. "I like the idea of eating flowers," she said. "Will you make them different colors?"

Richard looked at Jenny and rolled his eyes. He'd rather eat bugs.

"Yes, making the flowers colorful would be nice," said Susan.

Kevin raised his hand. "My cereal is Shark Attack!"

Everyone laughed. Except Richard, who stared at Kevin with his mouth open.

"That's very creative, Kevin," said Mrs. Steele. "Tell us about it."

"Each piece of cereal will be shaped like a shark," Kevin went on. "Then on the back of the box, there will be pictures of the different sharks and information about them."

Richard gasped. He'd been robbed. "Creative," yeah, right. It was *his* idea! He poked Kevin with his elbow.

"Ow," said Kevin, and poked him back.

Mrs. Steele gave Richard and Kevin the evil eye. Everyone in the class grew silent. Mrs. Steele continued to stare at them. Richard sat up straighter.

Finally, Mrs. Steele said, "Do you have an idea for your slogan yet?" she asked Kevin.

"Scare yourself," he said.

"Scare yourself awake in the morning," said Richard. If Kevin was going to steal his idea, he might as well steal it right.

Everyone laughed.

"Very catchy slogan, Richard," said Mrs. Steele. "Why don't you share your cereal idea with the class."

Richard read through his ideas again. He wasn't sure which one to pick now.

"Don't you have any ideas yet?" asked Mrs. Steele.

Everyone was silent, waiting for Richard to say something. Richard took a deep breath and read from his paper. "Crunchy Critters," he read, "bug friends in the shape of crickets, grasshoppers, and spiders." He looked up. Everyone was staring at him. "When soldiers get shot down, their survival manual tells them to eat insects."

"So you're thinking about having insects in your cereal?" said Mrs. Steele.

"Well, there already are insects in everyone's cereal," said Richard.

"No way!" said Jenny.

"I read about it on the Internet," said Richard. "Any time you eat a bowl of cereal, you probably eat about fifty insect fragments, too. Insects get into the grain before it's ground up. So I thought I'd add some insects like crickets to my cereal, ones that have lots of protein."

"That's disgusting," said Susan. Her curls bounced when she squirmed.

Kevin made retching sounds and covered his mouth.

Rana raised her hand. "In one part of India, people raise silkworms and then eat the silkworm pupae."

"Do people get bug breath when they eat bugs?" Kevin said.

"It's like dog breath, only worse," said Richard. He blew in Kevin's face, and Kevin fell over.

Mrs. Steele pursed her lips and looked at Kevin and Richard. No one moved. Then she turned to Rana. "That's very interesting," said Mrs. Steele. "I've heard about people eating insects in Asia and Africa." She looked at the clock. "It's time for recess, so get your coats and line up, except Kevin and Richard. I'd like to talk to you two boys before you go out."

Uh-oh, thought Richard.

While the rest of the class filed out of the room, Richard and Kevin stood by Mrs. Steele's desk. "I think you should apologize to Rana for being rude while she was talking," said Mrs. Steele.

Kevin made a sad clown face.

"Okay," said Richard.

"There's something else I want to suggest," said Mrs. Steele. "I would like you to be partners and help each other work on your cereal projects."

Richard's stomach lurched. "Work together?"

"Everyone in the class will be working with a buddy on this project," said Mrs. Steele. "I also want you to go to the supermarket together this weekend and fill out your cereal comparison sheets. I think working together will be good for both of you."

"I don't think I can help with Crunchy Critters," said Kevin. "The thought of eating insects makes me want to barf."

Richard groaned. The thought of working with Kevin made *him* want to barf.

Chapter 2

The next morning, Richard and Jenny stood together during recess.

"I read about honeypot ants from Australia last night," said Richard. "They store sweet stuff in their bellies. Aborigines eat them."

"I can't imagine eating ants." Jenny made a face. "Are you really going to use them for your cereal project?"

"I'm thinking about having a world map on the back of my cereal box," said Richard. "Then I could write about all the different insects people eat in different countries."

"So a lot of people eat insects?"

"Well, some do." Richard liked watching Jenny's face. When she looked really disgusted, she pushed her eyebrows together, nearly closing her eyes, and her mouth turned down. Way down.

A ball came skidding toward them. Jenny picked it up and tossed it back to a group of kids playing soccer.

"Look at that little kid over there." Jenny pointed toward an area of the playground called Tunnel Hill. "He's always alone."

Richard watched some kids crawling through the two tunnels. Then he saw a boy sitting by himself. "The kid with the glasses?"

Jenny nodded.

Just then, Kevin and two of his buddies stopped beside the kid and said something. The kid pulled his knees up, wrapped his arms around them, and put his head down.

"I wonder what Kevin said," said Richard.

"Nothing nice, I'm sure," said Jenny. "The poor kid looks like a turtle pulling into his shell."

"Kevin doesn't know how to be nice." Richard thought about how Kevin stole his cereal idea. *Mean* was the word that described Kevin.

They watched as Kevin walked away laughing. The kid looked sad.

After recess, Mrs. Steele had the class come to the front of the room and sit down. She pointed to the board. Under "Lunch Menu" someone had written "cockroach à la king."

Susan groaned and looked at Richard.

Mrs. Steele looked at him, too.

"I didn't do it," said Richard. He couldn't help smiling, though. It was kind of funny.

Mrs. Steele erased the offensive menu item. "Don't worry. The cafeteria is serving chicken à la king today."

Richard was glad he'd brought his lunch. He wondered if anyone in the class would eat the cafeteria food today.

"I have a surprise for you." Mrs. Steele picked up a shopping bag. "A friend of mine has given us a class pet."

"What is it?" asked Kevin. "A snake?"

Richard noticed that Kevin was wearing his snake shirt. Snakes were probably his favorite animal. Kevin was like a snake, one that struck without warning.

"No." Mrs. Steele sat down and took a plastic cage out of the bag. "This is a tarantula. A female tarantula." She pointed to a large spider that had climbed halfway up one side of the cage. "I'll let each of you get a closer look."

"I really like tarantulas," said Richard. "My next-door neighbor raises them."

"In his house?" Rana looked horrified.

"Sure," said Richard, "but they're all in plastic cages."

Jenny drew back when Mrs. Steele held the cage near her. "I'd rather have a rabbit," she said with a shiver.

"Or a guinea pig," said Rana. "Anything with fur."

"How about a nice baby tiger?" said Richard.

"Very funny, Richard," said Rana.

"Tarantulas are interesting," said Mrs. Steele. "They have adhesive pads on their feet, so they can walk up walls."

"That helps them escape from their cages," said Kevin.

Jenny grimaced.

"They like to hide in kids' desks," said Kevin. "When you least expect it, they jump out at you."

"That's quite enough of that kind of talk." Mrs. Steele looked sternly at Kevin. "The lid of the cage locks in place. The tarantula won't escape."

"She hopes it won't escape," Richard whispered, so only Jenny could hear him. He ran his fingers up Jenny's back like a galloping tarantula.

Jenny turned around and frowned at him.

Mrs. Steele set the cage on top of the bookshelf. Then she walked over to the blackboard. "Let's

come up with a list of questions about tarantulas."
She picked up a piece of chalk.

"How do you know it's a girl?" asked Rana.

"That's what I was told," said Mrs. Steele. "Female tarantulas live a lot longer than males."

"Is she poisonous?" asked Jenny.

"How long do tarantulas live?" asked Susan.

"What does she like to eat?" asked Rana.

"Tasty little girls," said Kevin with a smirk.

"Is it safe to hold her?" asked Jenny.

"I'm not really sure," said Mrs. Steele.

"I've held tarantulas a lot, but you have to be careful. If they rear up and strike out with their front legs, they're telling you to 'bug off!'" Richard said.

"Would you like to show us how to hold her?" asked Mrs. Steele.

"She might be stressed right now," said Richard. "It would be better to wait until next week."

"Where do tarantulas live?" asked Susan.

"Do they have enemies?" asked Jenny.

"How big do they get?" asked Kevin.

"Big enough to jump on your face," whispered Richard.

"Do they lay eggs?" asked Rana.

Mrs. Steele wrote all the questions on the board.

"Does she have a name?" asked Jenny.

"We can name her," said Mrs. Steele. "Any ideas? By the way, she's a Chilean rose tarantula."

"We could call her Rose," said Jenny. "But she doesn't look much like a flower."

"How about Spider Girl?" said Richard.

"Fang," said Kevin.

"Fang?" said Rana.

"Tarantulas have fangs, dummy," said Kevin.

"Kevin, could you say that again without the name-calling?" said Mrs. Steele.

"Tarantulas have fangs, Rana," said Kevin in a loud voice.

"Thank you, Kevin," said Mrs. Steele.

"Since she has pink on her, how about Ruby or Pinky?" said Susan.

"Let's vote on her name," said Mrs. Steele.

All the girls voted for Ruby. Most of the boys voted for Fang. A few voted for Spider Girl.

"Her name is officially Ruby," said Mrs. Steele.

Susan beamed.

"I'm not calling her Ruby," said Kevin in a low voice. "I'm calling her Fang!"

That didn't surprise Richard. Kevin did things his own way. If he did them at all.

Chapter 3

After lunch, Richard stopped by the boys' bathroom. Kevin and another boy were coming out as he entered. Richard noticed the little kid from the playground standing in one of the stalls as he walked by. A minute later, Richard looked in the mirror as he washed his hands and saw that the kid was still in the stall, standing still as a stone. "Are you okay?" he asked.

The kid didn't say anything.

Richard walked over to him. "Are you sick?"

The kid shook his head and then pointed into the toilet. A small toy truck had sunk to the bottom of the bowl.

"Want me to get it out of the water for you?" asked Richard.

"It's ruined," said the kid.

Richard leaned over. "It looks like a special waterproof truck to me. All it needs to do is start its jet engine and then it can zoom out of the water."

The kid looked at Richard with wide eyes.

"I'm Richard. What's your name?"

"Sam," said the kid.

"Well, Sam, here comes your truck, right out of the river and back onto the road." Richard knelt down, drove the truck out of the toilet bowl, and set it on the seat.

"But it's all dirty," said Sam.

"No problem." Richard stood up. "We'll take it to the car wash." He took the truck to the sink and rubbed soap all over it and over his hands and arms as well. "You should wash your hands really well if they were in the toilet."

Sam shook his head. "I didn't put my hands in there."

Richard rinsed the soap off, dried the truck with a paper towel, and handed it to Sam. "There it is, good as new."

"Thanks." Sam took the truck and smiled at Richard. "Your arms are still wet," he said, handing Richard another paper towel.

As Richard headed out to recess, he wondered how the truck had fallen into the toilet. Had the boy dropped it? Or had someone else parked the truck in the toilet bowl for him? Someone like Kevin.

That afternoon, Mrs. Steele read a book to them about tarantulas. "'Scientists have identified thirty-seven thousand different kinds of spiders. About eight hundred fifty of those are tarantulas. Tarantulas are larger than the rest of the spiders.'" Mrs. Steele looked up.

"Ruby's pretty big," said Jenny.

"Yes, she is," said Mrs. Steele. "But the biggest spider on earth is the goliath birdeater tarantula. Its leg span is twelve inches. Its fangs are an inch long." She held up a picture.

"I wouldn't want to find one of those crawling across my bed on a dark and stormy night," said Rana.

Jenny put her hands over her face and shivered.

"Do they really eat birds?" asked Susan.

"We'll add that to our list of questions," said Mrs. Steele. She continued reading. "'Tarantulas have eight eyes, but they can hardly see at all.'"

"Maybe they need glasses," said Kevin. He made circles with the thumb and index finger of each hand and put them up to his eyes.

Richard thought about Sam. What made Kevin pick on him? Was it because Sam had glasses?

Mrs. Steele read, "'Most tarantulas from North and South America protect themselves by kicking thousands of hairs off their abdomen at an enemy. These hairs are like small darts and are very irritating when they stick to the nose or eyes of an attacker.'"

"Does Ruby have hairs like that?" asked Susan.

"Yes," said Mrs. Steele.

Richard wished he had attack hairs. He'd flick a few at Kevin for stealing his cereal. He was sure Kevin had written the cockroach menu item on the board, too. Kevin was now making fun of Crunchy Critters. Richard had a new idea for his cereal box. He'd name the critters. The cockroach would be named Kevin.

"How many attack hairs does she have?" asked Jenny.

Mrs. Steele wrote Jenny's question on the board.

Mrs. Steele read more. "'Tarantulas rely almost entirely on touch, taste, and smell. They taste with special hairs on their feet and legs. Sense organs on their legs let them feel very faint vibrations that

tell them the size and location of an approaching insect. Like all spiders, they smell with their feet.'"

"Kevin has smelly feet, too," Richard said softly.

Kevin kicked him with a smelly foot.

Mrs. Steele looked at the clock and closed the book. "It's time to line up for music."

Richard stood up. At least in music class, he sat far away from Kevin.

Chapter 4

The next morning, Richard hurried into the classroom after the second bell had rung. Luckily, Mrs.
Steele was next door talking to another teacher.

As he passed the tarantula cage, he stopped.
Where was the tarantula? He couldn't see Ruby
anywhere. He stooped down and looked through
the side of the cage. Now, he could see inside the
flowerpot. Empty. Ruby was scrunched in the back
of the cage, by the flowerpot. She looked scared to
death. What was wrong with her?

"Bring your food journals up front," said Mrs.
Steele as she entered the classroom.

Richard grabbed his food journal from his backpack. He hadn't had a chance to fill it out. What
had he eaten for dinner? He checked his shirt for
clues. He'd worn the same shirt yesterday. There
was a brown spot on his stomach. It looked like

baked bean juice. Yes, they'd had hot dogs and beans for dinner. He rushed up the aisle and joined the rest of the class.

Several of the students were staring at the blackboard and snickering. There was a new item listed on the lunch menu: "scorpion stew."

Richard smiled. Had Kevin struck again? Or was someone else making fun of his insect project? Whoever it was had some great lunch ideas!

Mrs. Steele sat down. "First, I need to take a lunch count. Who's buying hot lunch today?"

No one raised a hand.

"No one is buying lunch today?"

Richard could tell his teacher was trying not to laugh.

"Okay, then. Let's talk about what you ate for breakfast."

Richard thought about saying poached ants on toast, but decided he'd better not. It would make everyone think he was responsible for the tasty lunch menu. Instead he asked, "Has the tarantula had any breakfast? She doesn't look very good. Do you think she's hungry?"

"I don't know, Richard," said Mrs. Steele. "Maybe she's not used to having so many people around. And she can feel all the vibrations in our classroom."

"It probably feels like giants are stomping around her cage," said Richard.

"I bet it does," said Mrs. Steele. "We'll discuss the tarantula later. Let's talk about human nutrition right now."

Jenny raised her hand. "I had cornflakes with a banana for breakfast."

Richard wished he'd had a bowl of cornflakes. He'd only had time to eat a piece of toast—without any poached ants. His stomach rumbled.

Mrs. Steele unrolled a chart and fastened it to the bulletin board. "This chart shows how much sugar is in a bowl of some popular cereals. How much sugar is in a bowl of cornflakes?"

"'Half a teaspoonful,'" Jenny read from the chart.

"That's right. So cornflakes would be a good choice, wouldn't it?"

"I had Grape-Nuts," said Susan. "That has no sugar."

"That's a good choice, too," said Mrs. Steele.

"I eat Pirate Crunch," said Kevin.

Gives you energy to torture little kids, Richard thought.

Mrs. Steele turned to the sugar chart. "Now, that's one of the cereals that has lots of sugar in it—four teaspoons in each serving."

"That's why I like it," said Kevin.

"What do the rest of you think about eating so much sugar for breakfast?"

"Sugar just provides empty calories," said Susan. "You should eat Grape-Nuts, Kevin."

"Grape-Nuts tastes like dog food," said Kevin.

"Have you ever eaten dog food?" asked Susan.

"Yes," said Kevin. "Arf, arf."

Even dog food sounded good to Richard. His stomach rumbled again.

"There's nothing wrong with eating some sugar," said Mrs. Steele. "We crave sugar because we need it. Sugar is a carbohydrate, and carbohydrates are the body's main source of fuel."

Kevin turned to Susan. "See!"

"At first, sugar gives you lots of energy. But when your sugar levels drop a few hours later, you might feel tired or even sleepy. Then you crave more sugar to get that energy boost."

"You are getting very sleepy, Kevin." Richard made his voice sound like a hypnotist's.

"So it's better to eat cereals without much sugar, right?" asked Susan, looking straight at Kevin.

"Well, you can still eat the sugary cereal if you eat only a little bit," said Mrs. Steele. "Mix the sugary cereal with another cereal, one that has less sugar."

"Mix a little Pirate Crunch with lots of Grape-Nuts," said Richard.

Kevin made a face. "Yuck!"

Mrs. Steele said, "The problem is that too much sweet stuff can make you fat."

"Kevin will turn into a fat pirate," Richard whispered.

Jenny stifled a laugh.

"I would never add any extra sugar to my food," said Susan.

"Cereals with lots of sugar tend to have less protein and fiber in them, too," said Mrs. Steele.

"Protein helps you grow," said Susan.

"Yes, and it gives you lots of energy," said Mrs. Steele. "What does fiber do for you?"

Nobody had a clue.

"It helps you go to the bathroom, doesn't it?" said Mrs. Steele. "If you don't get enough fiber, what happens to you?"

"You get plugged up," said Kevin.

"Correct," said Mrs. Steele. "You might get constipated."

Some of the kids laughed. Jenny rolled her eyes.

Richard wondered if Kevin's pirate cereal plugged him up. It would serve him right.

At lunch, Richard sat with Jenny. Susan joined them. Kevin sat several tables away with some friends from the other fourth-grade class. Richard opened his lunch box and removed his usual peanut butter and jelly sandwich from its plastic baggie. His stomach was rumbling like a thunderstorm now.

"Peanut butter again," said Susan.

"My favorite," said Richard.

"I bet the peanut butter company adds extra sugar to it," said Susan.

"My mother gets up early every morning to grind the peanuts for my sandwich," said Richard, "and she never adds sugar." He wiggled his eyebrows up and down.

Jenny laughed.

"Oh, right." Susan pinched her lips together. "Well, my lunch contains all the food groups." She held up her carrot sticks. Then an apple. "My sandwich is turkey with fresh greens on whole wheat bread. So that takes care of the meat group and the bread and cereal group." She opened her thermos and poured some milk into the lid. "And finally, the milk or dairy group."

"You forgot the fat group," said Richard.

"You only need one serving of that a day," said Susan.

"What about the sugar group?" asked Richard.

Susan acted like she hadn't heard his smart-alecky question.

Richard watched Kevin throw his balled-up lunch bag into the trash can from across the room. Good throw. It went in. Two points for Kevin's team.

Kevin and his buddies got up and walked out of the lunchroom together. A minute later, Kevin was back. He leaned over, stuck his arm deep into the lunch trash, then walked out. Very mysterious.

Richard punched the plastic bag and leftover crusts from his sandwich into a ball. "See you later," he said to Jenny and Susan. He stood up. A kid was now standing on tiptoe with his head inside the trash can. It was Sam, the little boy with the glasses. Then the trash can fell over.

Richard looked for help, but the lunchroom aide was busy with a kid who'd dropped his tray. She hadn't seen what happened.

Richard hurried over to the trash can. He heard the muffled sound of crying. Richard knelt down, pulled the kid out of the can, and helped him sit up. Tears rolled down Sam's cheeks. Richard put his arm around the boy. "What's happened?" he asked.

Sam's lower lip trembled. "They took my glasses. The bad guy threw my glasses in the trash." He took a long, shaking breath. "I can't find them."

"Let's look together," said Richard. He pulled more trash out of the can. He leaned far inside, feeling under crumpled paper and half-eaten sandwiches and milk cartons for the missing glasses. He touched something squishy and slimy and grimaced as he pulled out a banana peel. Holding it up, he said, "Are these your glasses?" Richard put the banana skin on his nose.

"No." Sam almost smiled.

Richard reached into the can again. This time, he pulled out a small pair of black-rimmed glasses. "How about these?" Richard looked through the glasses. "You're all fuzzy."

"No, *you're* fuzzy," said Sam with a smile.

"You have some red spots, too." Richard took off the glasses and studied them. "Hmm, tomato sauce." He wiped the glasses with a napkin.

Sam reached for his glasses and put them on. "You're not fuzzy anymore."

"Whew, that's a relief," said Richard. "If I went

back to class looking fuzzy, my friends might mistake me for our tarantula."

"You have a tarantula?" Sam opened his eyes so wide he looked bug-eyed.

"She's our class pet," said Richard. "And guess what? She has eight eyes."

"I bet nobody ever teases a tarantula about her eyes," said Sam. "Those bad guys call me a four-eyed nose-wipe." He hiccuped back a sob.

"That's really mean," said Richard. "If you were a tarantula, nobody would dare make fun of you. Tarantulas can fight back with special darts on their tummies. The darts make people itch."

"Wow," said Sam. "I wish I had magic darts."

"Somebody I know deserves some darts shot into his butt," said Richard.

"Who?" asked Sam, but he started to smile.

"Kevin, otherwise known as Mr. Bully-butt." Richard grinned, and Sam grinned back.

Chapter 5

Richard got up early on Friday. He just had to get through the day, then he'd have a great weekend to look forward to. A weekend with no Kevin or Sam to worry about. He ate a big breakfast: half a grapefruit, scrambled eggs, a whole wheat muffin with a tiny bit of jam, and milk. It was the kind of breakfast that Susan would brag about. Richard took out his food journal and wrote down each thing he ate and its food group. With plenty of protein and fiber in his body, Richard set out to conquer the world.

The air outside was damp and cold. Richard exhaled, and his breath turned to steam. He looked up at the thick, gray clouds. Maybe it would snow.

In the next block, a small figure was plodding to school. It looked a bit like Sam, but Richard couldn't tell from behind. He walked faster. He watched as Kevin and two of his evil sidekicks crossed the street and stood in front of the boy. Richard started to walk even faster. He watched as Kevin grabbed the kid's lunch box.

"That's my lunch," wailed the small kid.

Bully-butt was striking again. Richard started running.

"Hi, Sam," said Richard, puffing and blowing steam. He put his hand on Sam's shoulder. His heart was thudding inside his chest. "Hi, Kevin."

"Is this four-eyed nose-wipe a friend of yours?" asked Kevin.

"Yes, he is," said Richard.

"We're the nutrition police," Kevin said, "and we're trying to help the little nerd eat better." He held up a large brownie in a plastic bag, then glared at Sam. "This is so bad for you! Too much sugar! I'm taking it away for your own good."

"Kevin, you're a bonehead," said Richard.

"And you're a nose-wipe, just like your little friend." Kevin put the brownie in his pocket, closed the lunch box, and gave it back to Sam. The lunch box had tigers on it.

All Richard could do was stare at Kevin. He wished he were a tiger. He'd growl and bash Kevin and get the brownie back. Instead, he just watched

as Kevin crossed the street with his gang. They were all laughing.

"My mom made that brownie for me," said Sam.

"Would it help if I walked you to school in the morning?" asked Richard.

Sam looked doubtful. "Maybe."

"I could put your lunch box in my backpack," said Richard.

"He'd still call me bad names," said Sam.

"But at least he couldn't get your brownie," said Richard.

Sam looked up at him. "There are three of them and only one of you."

So much for conquering the world. He couldn't even stop Kevin from stealing a little kid's brownie.

When Richard got to the classroom, Kevin was already in his seat. He smirked at Richard. "Nose-wipe," he said softly.

"Bully-butt," said Richard.

Mrs. Steele looked up from her desk. Uh-oh. She stood up. And she wasn't smiling. "I've overheard some of you talking unkindly to each other." She looked around the room. Her eyes settled on Kevin momentarily, then moved on to Richard.

"Starting right now, we are going to work on being kind to one another," Mrs. Steele continued.

"Give me an example of something positive or kind you could say to one of your classmates," said Mrs. Steele.

Susan's hand shot into the air.

"Yes, Susan," said Mrs. Steele.

"When someone helps you with your homework or lends you a pencil, you could say, 'Thank you very much.'"

"Nice, Susan," said Mrs. Steele. "And be sure to use the person's name."

"If Kevin did something nice, I would say, 'Thank you very much, Kevin.'"

Richard snorted. "That'll be the day," he said softly.

"Do you have something to add, Richard?" said Mrs. Steele.

"I just love your snake shirt, Kevin," said Richard in a girlish voice. "It looks so real. Real enough to bite." Richard thought about putting a snake in Kevin's desk. A big one. The thought of it made him smile.

"Anyone else?" asked Mrs. Steele.

Kevin raised his hand. "Richard, your dirty tennis shoes smell so good."

Mrs. Steele frowned. "Now, I want you to be serious about this."

Jenny raised her hand. "If someone is having a hard time doing math questions, you could offer to help."

"Yes," said Mrs. Steele. "That would be kind."

"And if someone is having trouble drawing something on their cereal box," said Susan, "you could offer to help them."

"That would be kind, as well," said Mrs. Steele. "I want you to be thinking about kind and caring things you can do for one another. When you start to say something negative or mean to someone, stop yourself and say something kind instead. Can someone give me an example of that?"

Susan raised her hand again. "Maybe someone is making a very messy drawing, and you're about to say, 'That looks awful.'" Susan took a breath. "Instead you should say, 'Gosh, it looks like you're having trouble. Can I help?'"

"Very good, Susan," said Mrs. Steele.

Kevin put his head down on his desk.

Mrs. Steele picked up a stack of papers from her desk. "I'm handing out a work sheet for you to use when you visit the cereal aisle of a grocery store. Try to go with your partner this weekend, if possible."

Richard looked at the work sheet. It was two pages long, and there were lots of questions. He'd have to spend hours looking at cereal boxes with Kevin. His weekend was ruined.

"Right now, I want you to work on your cereal project with your partner," said Mrs. Steele. "Don't use any put-downs. Think about being kind and positive."

Richard got out his papers. Then he looked at Kevin. "Dear Kevin," he said, "shall we get to work?"

Jenny looked up and chuckled.

"Oh, yes, kind Richard," said Kevin. "I can't wait." He got out a single sheet of paper and let his desk lid slam shut.

"Do you want to go to the store on Saturday afternoon?" Richard held up the sheet of questions.

"I'd love to spend Saturday afternoon in the cereal aisle with you," said Kevin. "Who needs to watch a silly football game? Cereal boxes are so much more exciting."

Chapter 6

After recess, Mrs. Steele called everyone to the front of the room. She sat in her rocking chair. On the table beside her was the tarantula cage.

"I went to the pet store last night and bought some crickets." She pulled a small plastic cage from a bag. "We'll offer some to Ruby." She set the crickets next to the tarantula cage. The crickets were climbing on top of one another, leaping around, and chirping.

"So Ruby eats crickets?" asked Rana.

"Yes," said Mrs. Steele. "And she likes them alive and moving around."

"Ick," said Rana.

Richard laughed and pointed to the board.

Mrs. Steele looked around, then she saw the lunch menu. Today someone had written, "chirpy cricket tacos."

"Cricket tacos. I think Ruby would like one." Mrs. Steele smiled. "The man in the pet store said she might eat eight crickets a week, so I bought two dozen."

"That would be enough for three weeks," said Susan.

Richard gave Susan a dirty look. She was being a show-off as usual.

"That's right," said Mrs. Steele. "But then I read in one book that a tarantula might eat three crickets a week, and in another book that she might eat only one a week."

"Are we going to keep track of how many she eats?" asked Susan.

"Yes," said Mrs. Steele. "Then we can see how much it costs to feed Ruby compared to a dog or cat or hamster."

"Of course feeding Ruby will be much cheaper than feeding a dog or cat." Susan had a smug look on her face.

"It could be," said Mrs. Steele. "The crickets cost only eight cents each." Mrs. Steele took the lid off the tarantula cage. Ruby was sitting inside the flowerpot. She didn't move. Mrs. Steele opened the cricket cage and reached for a pair of tongs. "I'm going to try to pick up a cricket without squashing it." While she tried to capture a cricket, it jumped out of the cage onto the table. Then the cricket jumped to the floor.

Richard crawled after the cricket. He was surprised that all the crickets didn't try to leap away. But maybe they didn't know they were destined to be spider food. Richard finally caught up to the cricket and cupped his hand over it. "Shall I give this one to the tarantula?" he asked.

"Yes, go ahead," said Mrs. Steele.

Richard scooped up the cricket and dumped it into the cage. Ruby still didn't move.

Mrs. Steele finally caught another cricket with the tongs and dropped it in as well. Then she put the lid on the tarantula's cage.

One cricket jumped behind Ruby's flowerpot. The other one stayed still. Then it jumped toward the water bowl. In a flash, Ruby ran out and grabbed that one. She held it underneath her body, by her mouth.

"Wow! Ruby can move fast when she wants to," said Jenny.

"The poor cricket!" said Rana. "Ruby grabbed its body with those two short legs by her head."

"Those are called pedipalps," said Mrs. Steele. "They are her food-handling feet."

"I wonder how long it will take for her to eat that cricket?" asked Richard.

"That's an interesting question," said Mrs. Steele. "How can we figure that out?"

"I guess we could time her," said Richard.

"Let's do that," said Mrs. Steele. She wrote the time on the board. Next to the time, she wrote, "Catches cricket."

Richard was pleased with himself.

"We're going to the library in a few minutes," said Mrs. Steele. "You can look for information about tarantulas, as well as anything you might need for your cereal project."

"But what about timing how fast Ruby eats her lunch?" asked Richard.

"I'll stay here and do that," said Susan. "I went to the public library a few days ago, so I have all the books I need."

Susan was always ahead of everyone else. She liked to brag about it, too.

When Richard got to the library, he went over to Nando, the librarian. Kevin followed him. Nando had a ponytail and could speak Spanish as well as English, because he had grown up in Mexico. "What can I do for you, amigos?" he said.

"I need a book on sharks," said Kevin.

Nando led them to the computer. "We have several shark books, and they all have the call number 597.31. The nonfiction books are over there." He pointed to the shelves, then went off to help other students.

"Let's go," said Kevin.

"Wait," said Richard, "I want to find the numbers for my books." He started typing.

"Hurry up," said Kevin, "before I forget my number. I think it's five hundred ninety. Or maybe nine hundred fifty."

Richard sighed loudly, typed in "sharks," and wrote down the number. Then he went to the shelves and picked out the first shark book he saw, thrusting it at Kevin.

While Kevin paged through the book, Richard went back to look up crickets and tarantulas.

"Watch out," Jenny yelled.

Richard looked up. Kevin had his book open and was chasing Mike, another boy from their class. "A great white shark is going to eat you!" Kevin kept jabbing Mike with the book. Mike turned around and hit Kevin with his book. Now they were pretending that their books were swords. With a mighty whack, Kevin knocked the book out of Mike's hand.

Nando rushed past. "Gentlemen, this is not how

you treat library books." He took the books from
both boys. "Return to your classroom right now."

Richard gritted his teeth. His partner was in
trouble again. Now, Kevin didn't have any information about sharks. Well, that was just too bad. Why
should Richard care if Kevin couldn't finish his
project? Kevin often didn't finish his homework.
Except that Richard was Kevin's partner. And
Mrs. Steele had just lectured them on being kind.
Richard hurried after Nando.

"I'll take the shark book," said Richard. "We're
supposed to be kind to our classmates today."

"Make sure your classmate is kind to our library books." Nando handed him the book.

"I'm having trouble finding anything about eating insects," said Richard.

"That's a good subject," said Nando. "Have you ever had a grasshopper taco?"

Richard shook his head. "Are they like cricket tacos?"

"They're both tasty," said Nando. "Of course, people in this country think you're crazy if you eat insects. But that's not true in some places in Mexico." Nando led Richard to the computer in his office. "Let's see what Google can find for you."

Richard was surprised at how many items the search engine found when he entered "eating insects." He scanned down the list and clicked on "cricket brownies." A recipe for making brownies appeared on the screen. The brownies had crickets in them. And he thought of a disgusting but wonderful plan.

Right after school, Richard found Sam in his classroom. "I'm going to put crickets in your brownies," he told Sam.

Sam looked horrified.

"Not for you to eat," explained Richard. "For Kevin."

"He might beat me up," said Sam.

"I'll protect you," said Richard. "Now let's get some crickets."

"Are we going to catch them?" asked Sam.

"We're going to take two of Ruby's crickets," said Richard.

"Who's Ruby?" asked Sam.

"Our tarantula," said Richard as he led Sam down the hall. When they reached the fourth-grade classroom, Richard was glad to find no one there. He didn't think Mrs. Steele would like his plan to get even with Mr. Bully-butt. He showed Sam the tarantula. Ruby was sitting right outside her flowerpot.

"Wow! She's big!" said Sam. "And very hairy. Where are the darts she can throw at people?"

"On her tummy," said Richard.

"Can I hold her?" asked Sam.

"I haven't held her yet, but we can try." Richard moved the tarantula cage to the floor. He and Sam sat down beside it. "Well, now's our chance." Richard took the lid off the cage and moved his hand near Ruby. The tarantula stood on her back

legs and waved her pedipalps. Richard removed his hand. Quickly.

"Why is she doing that?" asked Sam.

"She threatened me by showing her fangs." Richard put the lid back on the cage. "She's letting us know that she doesn't want to be bothered today. If I try to pick her up now, she might bite me."

"She's very brave," said Sam. "I bet even Mr. Bully-butt wouldn't mess with her!"

Richard laughed. "Let's get two crickets, and then I'll walk you home." He put the tarantula cage back on the shelf. He took a small plastic bag out of his backpack. There was a cookie inside. He gave half to Sam and stuffed the other half into his mouth. "Here, hold the bag open." Richard handed the empty bag to Sam, then picked up the tongs and grabbed a cricket. He put the cricket in the bag. "Don't let him jump out." Sam closed the bag. Richard picked up another cricket, and Sam held the bag open. "I'll bake them first, then put them inside a brownie."

Richard put the bag of crickets in his backpack. He hoped Mrs. Steele wouldn't notice the missing crickets.

"But I don't have any more brownies at my house," said Sam. "Mr. Bully-butt ate the last one."

"I'll make some this weekend and bring you one on Sunday," said Richard. "You can pack it in your lunch box."

"Then Mr. Bully-butt will steal it, right?" Sam looked up at Richard.

"I sure hope so," said Richard. "And when he eats it, he'll get a big, crunchy surprise."

Chapter 7

After finishing his lunch on Saturday, Richard started reading the book his mother had brought home for him. The title was *Strange Foods: Bush Meat, Bats, and Butterflies*. It was handy to have a mother who was a research librarian at the local college. He read the section on spiders and scorpions first. "'Some spiders can make a lovely meal,'" he read out loud to his mother, who was reading the paper. "'Especially tarantulas. In Laos and Cambodia, people like to eat the blue-legged tarantula.'"

"To each his own," said his mother, shaking her head. "What do tarantulas taste like?"

Richard turned the page. "Let's see. The author says they taste like a combination of almond and chicken bone marrow. Do you want one for dinner?"

"Plain chicken would do nicely," said his mother.

"Where's your sense of adventure?" asked Richard.

"I'm ready for our adventure in the cereal aisle." She picked up his questionnaire. "Gee, this could take a while."

"Wait till you meet Kevin." Richard put on his coat. "That's an adventure in itself."

"I can't wait," said his mother.

"While you're shopping," said Richard, "could you get some brownie mix? But don't let Kevin see it."

"The plot thickens," said his mother.

Richard smiled. How did his mother always know when he was up to something?

After picking up Kevin, they drove to the grocery store. Once there, Kevin insisted on taking his own cart to the cereal aisle.

"I don't think we need a cart," said Richard. "We're looking, not buying."

But Kevin ignored him and raced off, pushing the cart. He careened down the nearest aisle, then stood on the cart and rode for a short distance before crashing into a cart filled with cans and boxes.

"Watch out, sonny," said a lady as she bent to pick up a package of toilet paper.

"Sorry," said Richard as Kevin disappeared around the corner. He caught up with Kevin in the cereal aisle. It was crowded with shoppers.

"Now what?" said Kevin.

"Well, if you've run over enough little old ladies," said Richard, opening his notebook, "we can work on our cereal questions."

Kevin snorted.

Richard read, "'How many cereals are there?'"

Kevin looked up and down the aisle. "Hundreds. We don't have to count them, do we?"

"It's one of the questions," said Richard.

"You count them." Kevin yawned.

Richard shook his head. Just as he'd suspected, he'd have to do all the work. He'd count them later. He read more questions out loud. "'Which cereals do you want to buy? What attracted you to them? The name, bright colors on the box, or prizes in the box?'"

Kevin yawned again.

Richard walked slowly down the aisle.

Kevin followed him.

Richard stopped, picked up a box, read the back and front, and then wrote in his notebook.

Kevin peered over his shoulder. "What does that say?"

"I wrote down the slogan: 'Crackling little *Os*.' Then I said I like the colors."

"Oh," said Kevin.

"Pick out a cereal that you like," said Richard.

"That's easy," said Kevin. "Pirate Crunch."

"And what attracts you to that cereal?" asked Richard.

"It tastes good."

"Before you ever tasted it," said Richard, "what would have attracted you to the box?"

"I like pirates."

Richard read from the sheet Mrs. Steele handed out. "'Find the list of ingredients.'"

Kevin picked up the box. "Look, there's a new game on the back. I haven't played this one yet."

Richard grabbed the box from him and found the ingredient list. "We're supposed to see what grains are listed."

Kevin grabbed the box back. "'Corn flour,'" he read. "Is that a grain?"

"I guess." Richard wrote "corn flour" on the sheet. "What sugars are there?"

"Sugar," said Kevin.

"Just plain sugar?" Richard looked closely at the side of the box.

"Yep," said Kevin. "Then oat flour is next. And after that brown sugar."

"Okay, so there are two sugars—sugar and brown sugar." Richard wrote those down. "And oat flour is a grain."

"I knew that." Kevin gave him a dirty look. He picked up another cereal box and looked at the back. "This one has a maze."

Richard walked slowly past box after box of cereal. He noticed that a few cereals had prizes inside. He looked at the colors of the boxes. "I think I like the bright red boxes best," he said.

"I like the green boxes," said Kevin.

Richard went back to the beginning of the aisle and started counting the different cereals.

"Can we go now?" Kevin raced up the aisle and jumped onto his cart.

"Kevin," Richard called after him. "You help me count these cereals. Or I'm going to tell Mrs. Steele that I did all the work."

Kevin left the cart and walked toward Richard. "What do you want me to do?"

"Start counting at the other end of the aisle, and we'll meet in the middle," said Richard. "Then we'll add our cereal counts together."

Kevin scowled, but he walked to the end of the aisle. And now he was actually pointing at each individual cereal and moving his lips.

Richard was surprised. He'd told Kevin what to do, and Kevin was doing it.

Chapter 8

On Sunday afternoon, Richard made brownies.

"Are you making brownies for someone special?" His mother handed him a glass dish and turned on the oven.

"Yes," said Richard.

"A girlfriend?" His mother picked some eggshell fragments out of the batter.

"No way." Richard made a face.

"Who then?" His mother folded her arms across her chest. She wasn't giving up.

"For Sam." Richard put his nose over the bowl and breathed in the chocolaty smell. "Mmm, smell this."

But his mother ignored him and continued her questions. "Is Sam a new boy in your class? You've never mentioned him before."

"He's a new kid in second grade." Richard poured the batter into the baking dish.

"How did you get to know him?"

"I'm helping him with a problem."

"What kind of problem?"

"A bully is stealing his brownies." Richard slid the dish into the oven.

"That's very nice of you to help him," said his mother. "Does his teacher know about the bully?"

"I don't think so," said Richard.

"Maybe you should talk to your teacher about it." His mother took the mixing bowl and put it in the sink.

"I don't want to be a snitch."

"I understand that," said his mother. "But your teacher might have some good suggestions."

"Maybe." Richard set a timer.

After the brownies were baked, Richard worked on the next part of the plan. He got on the Internet and entered, "cooking crickets."

Richard was amazed that there was so much information about it. After reading several recipes, he printed one out. He called his mother back to the kitchen to help him set the oven temperature to two hundred degrees. "This recipe says to cook the crickets on a cookie sheet. Do I need to grease it first?"

"No," said his mother, "I don't think so." She looked a little puzzled.

Richard took the crickets out of the freezer and placed them on a cookie sheet. The recipe promised that they would have a nutty flavor when cooked. Not that he cared what they tasted like. He wasn't going to eat them.

"Are those crickets for your friend, too?" his mother asked.

Richard had to think fast. "They're an experiment for my cereal project."

His mother raised her eyebrows.

"Insects are the food of the future," said Richard.

"Yummy," said his mother.

After the crickets had spent an hour in the oven, Richard took them out. He spread frosting on the

brownies, then cut them up. He selected a nice-looking brownie and buried the two crickets in the frosting. After covering the crickets with more frosting, he studied the brownie. No cricket parts were sticking out. He placed the brownie in a sandwich bag. Then he put on his coat and walked the three blocks to Sam's house. Sam promised to put the special brownie in his lunch box. If the bully struck on Monday morning, he'd get some extra protein with his brownie. Maybe a cricket leg would get stuck in his teeth. Just the thought of it made Richard smile.

On Monday, Richard got to school early. He stood next to Jenny and waited for Sam. Would Kevin steal the brownie? Maybe he was sick today. Maybe he was tired of stealing brownies from little kids.

Finally, Sam appeared. He rushed up to Richard. "Bully-butt took my brownie."

"Great," said Richard.

Sam grinned, then ran over to line up with his class.

"Why is that great?" asked Jenny.

"Because he'll get a big surprise," said Richard.

"What did you do?"

"I put two baked crickets inside the brownie," said Richard.

"Bad idea," said Jenny. "Kevin will blame Sam. Maybe he'll even beat Sam up."

"I'm going to walk Sam to school and home again," said Richard.

"Forever?" asked Jenny.

Richard shrugged. Maybe his plan wasn't that great.

When Mrs. Steele asked who was having hot lunch, everyone laughed. Today, the lunch menu item on the board was "stinkbug soup."

The class spent most of the morning working on its cereal projects. Susan had used a real cereal box. She had pasted green paper on each side of the original box. Then she made flowers out of red, pink, and yellow paper. Now she was putting the finishing touches on the back of her cereal box.

"That looks great, Susan," said Rana.

Susan beamed. She and Rana were partners.

Rana turned to Richard. "Let me see the front of your box."

Richard didn't want to show anyone his project yet, but he held up a piece of paper.

"'Crunchy Critters,'" Rana read. "'The nutty flavor of real roasted crickets'? Are you sure you want to use real bugs?"

"Bugs contain lots of protein to make you grow strong," he said. "Just ask Ruby."

"Tarantulas like bugs," said Susan, "but people don't."

"People in other countries eat insects," said Richard. "And there's a company in California that makes a lollipop with a cricket inside."

"That's gross," said Susan.

Richard was discouraged. His cereal idea was a flop.

Kevin thrust a piece of paper onto Richard's desk. "I need help drawing sharks," he said.

"Find the library book I gave you about sharks," Richard said sharply. First he'd thought of the idea. Now Kevin wanted him to draw the sharks.

Kevin searched through his desk and pulled out the book. "Draw one of the scary sharks. I like the ones that kill people."

"That figures," said Richard. "Okay, I'll draw the great white." He studied the picture, then drew the shark. "Wow, the great white has three thousand teeth!"

"Where does it say that?" asked Kevin.

"Right here." Richard pointed to the sentence in the book.

Kevin underlined it with his pencil.

"You're not supposed to write in library books." Richard pushed Kevin's hand away.

Kevin glared at him. "I was afraid I couldn't find the sentence later."

"Write it under the picture right now."

"What should I write?" asked Kevin.

"The great white shark has three thousand teeth."

Kevin wrote under the picture, then paged through the book. "Now draw a tiger shark for me," he said.

"You can draw that one yourself." Richard was tired of doing Kevin's work for him.

"I tried. My sharks look like bananas," said Kevin.

Richard gritted his teeth. "Too bad."

Jenny said, "I'll show you how to use tracing paper, Kevin." She took a piece of tracing paper from her desk and helped Kevin transfer the tiger shark picture to his cereal box.

Richard smiled at Jenny. She was being kind to Kevin. Or maybe she was being kind to him. He wondered if Kevin had eaten the cricket brownie yet. Probably not. He was in too good a mood. Unless the crickets tasted so good he didn't realize he was eating bugs.

At lunch, Richard sat where he could watch Kevin.

"Who are you staring at?" Jenny was sitting beside him.

"Kevin." Richard picked up his sandwich and took a big bite. He watched Kevin chew his sandwich.

Susan turned to look at Kevin. "He's chewing," she said. "Big deal."

"I'm waiting for him to eat his dessert," said Richard.

Jenny giggled.

Susan and Rana both turned to watch Kevin.

"Don't let him see you looking at him," said Richard. "He might get suspicious."

"Suspicious about what?" asked Rana.

"Hang on a second. I'll tell you if there's something worth looking at." Richard watched as Kevin picked up another piece of his sandwich. "His sandwich is cut into little triangles. How sweet."

"If you cut your sandwich into smaller pieces," said Susan, "you might not have jelly dripping on your shirt."

Richard looked at his shirt and rolled his eyes. "Okay. Kevin's finished with the sandwich at last. What will he eat next? He reaches into his lunch bag. He pulls something out. Don't look at him. But yes, I think he's got a brownie in his hand. He holds it out for his buddies to look at. They laugh."

Both Susan and Rana had stopped eating.

"Okay, he raises the brownie to his mouth. He's taking a bite. Yes, fans, he's eating the brownie."

"Can we look yet?" Rana took a quick peek over her shoulder.

"No, not yet," said Richard. "One of his buddies tries to take the brownie. Kevin shoves him away and takes a big bite. He's chewing. Yes, he's chewing. He stops chewing. Now he's poking the brownie."

"What's with this brownie?" Susan stole a glance at Kevin.

"Now he sees it. It's a horrible sight. There are mutilated cricket bodies inside the frosting." Richard clutched his throat. By now, everyone at his lunch table was staring at Kevin. Richard continued his narration anyway. "Kevin throws the brownie down. His face is red. He's looking around the lunchroom. Uh-oh, now he's staring at me. His beady eyes have turned mean. I think he suspects I might have had something to do with this terrible deed." Richard looked away. He was so proud of himself, he could not help smiling. His plan had worked.

"He looks mad," said Jenny.

"Did you really put crickets in a brownie?" asked Susan.

"Yes, I did, and I'm glad."

When Richard looked up again, Kevin was leaving the lunchroom.

"I think I'll need some help walking Sam home tonight," said Richard.

"Why?" asked Susan.

"Bully-butt will probably come after him," said Richard.

"You mean Kevin," said Susan.

Richard nodded.

"I'll come with you," said Jenny.

"Me, too," said Rana.

"I wish I could come, but I have a piano lesson," said Susan.

"That's okay," said Richard.

After school, Jenny and Rana walked with Richard to Sam's classroom.

"Did Bully-butt eat the brownie?" asked Sam.

"Yes," said Richard. "It all went exactly as we'd planned."

Sam was wide-eyed. "Was he mad?"

"Yes," said Jenny. "His face got red, and he slammed the brownie on the table."

"Uh-oh," said Sam. "He's going to get me."

"Don't worry," said Richard. "I'll protect you."

"We'll all walk you to school tomorrow," said Jenny.

There was no sign of Kevin or his friends as they escorted Sam home. After Sam had gone inside his house, Richard said, "I have a new plan. Let's all meet here tomorrow morning wearing glasses."

"What good will that do?" asked Rana.

"Kevin teases Sam about his glasses and calls him a four-eyed nose-wipe," explained Richard. "But if we all wear glasses, Sam won't feel so bad. Besides, Kevin might back off if we make fun of his name-calling."

Chapter 9

The next morning, Richard was running late. He had forgotten to find a pair of glasses the day before, and now all he could find was a pair from Halloween with a big nose and a mustache. That would have to do. As he ran out his front door, he grabbed his backpack and wished he could fly. Instead, he had to run all the way to Sam's house.

Jenny and Rana were already there, waiting with Sam.

"I thought you forgot about me," Sam said.

"No way," said Richard. "Sometimes I have trouble getting out of bed in the morning."

"You do?" said Sam. "I like to get up early."

"When you get older, like me," said Richard, "you have to sleep a lot, because growing big is tiring."

Sam stared up at Richard, with a questioning look on his face. "Really?"

"Really." Richard smiled and winked. He pulled out his glasses and put them on.

Jenny put on a pair of thin, gold-rimmed glasses. "They're my mother's old reading glasses," she explained. She wore them halfway down her nose and peered over the top.

"All I could find were my little sister's sunglasses," said Rana. She put them on. They were orange with tiger stripes. There were tigers above each lens.

"We all look so cool in our glasses," said Richard.

"I like the tiger glasses best," said Sam. He grinned.

The walk to school was uneventful. No hideous monsters were hiding in the bushes. No slimy ogres climbed out of the sewers. Maybe the cricket brownie had taught the bully a lesson.

Kevin was already at school when Richard and the rest of Sam's security force arrived. He looked up at them, but didn't react when he saw their eyewear.

Richard sat down and looked at the board for the latest lunch menu item. It was "cricket patties on a bun." Kevin had to be the person writing these buggy items on the lunch menu every day. Richard pointed to the board and Jenny laughed.

During reading and math, Kevin was unusually quiet. He even stayed in during recess to work on his cereal project. This was a different Kevin.

At lunch, Richard sat with Jenny. Susan and Rana joined them as usual. Kevin sat nearby with his friends. Richard opened his lunch box and removed his peanut butter and jelly sandwich from its plastic baggie. His stomach was rumbling.

"Peanut butter again," said Susan.

"My favorite," said Richard. He took a bite, chewed once or twice, then spit a wad of mashed bread and peanut butter onto the table. He peered at the partially eaten sandwich in his hand, then pulled the two pieces of bread apart. Several crickets were stuck in the peanut butter. One cricket was missing its head. He held the sandwich out for Jenny and Susan to see.

Susan made a gagging sound, put her hand to her mouth, and turned away.

"You aren't going to finish that, are you?" said Jenny.

"I'd be glad to share," said Richard. "Anyone?" He offered the sandwich to Rana. "It's yummy."

"Grow up," said Susan. She'd recovered quickly from her gagging attack.

Richard looked at Kevin. Kevin smirked. It was a bad-guy smirk. Richard smiled back. "I should just go ahead and eat the crickets, but I'm not sure if Kevin prepared them properly."

"How do you prepare a cricket for eating?" asked Jenny.

"If you catch it in a field somewhere, you have to let it eat something good like an orange slice for twenty-four hours. Then you should bake it in the oven to bring out the nutty flavor."

"So you don't think the crickets on your sandwich were cooked properly?" Jenny studied the headless cricket.

"No." Richard pointed to the cricket that still had a head. "This cricket is still moving."

Rana groaned and covered her eyes with her hands.

Richard put his sandwich back into the plastic bag, squished it into a ball, and tossed it toward the trash can. It was a tough shot, but the balled-up sandwich hit the rim and dropped into the can. "Yes!"

Jenny rolled her eyes and passed him half of her sandwich.

Someone tapped on his arm. It was Sam. "I need you," Sam said.

"Duty calls." Richard stood up. "Potty break?" he asked.

Sam nodded.

Stuffing the rest of Jenny's sandwich into his mouth, Richard followed Sam out of the lunchroom. He wondered how many times a day Sam visited the bathroom. Sam was small. Maybe his bladder was small, too. While Sam used the toilet, Richard stared at himself in the mirror. This bodyguard thing could seriously interfere with his life.

Chapter 10

The following day, Richard, Jenny, and Rana walked Sam to school. Once again, they all wore their glasses. They didn't run into Kevin. He must have overslept, because he was late getting to class. Mrs. Steele had already taken roll. Kevin slunk to his seat like a dog that had been beaten.

Richard noticed that the lunch menu hadn't been changed from the day before. Now he was sure that Kevin had been writing those menu items on the board. But the names of the dishes were so clever. Kevin couldn't have made them up. It was still very mysterious.

They were all working on a math work sheet when there was a knock at the door. Richard watched while Mrs. Steele walked over and opened it. A boy about the same size as Sam spoke to her.

"Richard, could you come here?" said Mrs. Steele.

Richard got up slowly. Now what? This little kid had glasses, too. He hoped this wasn't another little kid who needed protection in the bathroom.

"Do you know Daniel?" asked Mrs. Steele.

Richard shook his head.

"Richard, this is Daniel. He wants you to go to the boys' room with him, because Sam is there and refuses to go back to class."

Daniel grabbed Richard's hand. "Come on."

"Maybe I should come, too," said Mrs. Steele.

"No, Sam only wants Richard," said Daniel.

Richard hurried after Daniel, who was practically running down the hall. "What happened to Sam?"

"He's really upset," said Daniel. "You'll see."

As they entered the bathroom, Richard could hear sobbing. He rushed to the closed door of one of the stalls. "Sam, is that you?"

"Yes." Sam's voice was shaky.

"Open the door," said Richard.

Sam fumbled with the latch and slowly opened the door. Sam's face was wet from crying.

Richard could see the problem right away. Between Sam's nose and upper lip, someone had drawn a big green mustache.

"I tried to wash it off," said Sam.

"Did Kevin do this?" asked Richard, kneeling down.

Sam nodded. He sobbed some more.

"I think it's a beautiful mustache," said Richard, "and I'd like one just like it."

"Me, too," said Daniel.

Sam looked up. "You're just saying that."

"No, I'm not just saying it," said Richard. "I'll go back to my classroom to get a green marking pen. You can wait here if you want."

Richard rushed off. As soon as he came back, he drew a mustache on Daniel's face. Then he looked in the mirror and drew one on his own face. "There. How do you like our mustaches, Sam?"

"Okay, I guess," said Sam.

"Now let's go back to your classroom." Richard took Sam's hand.

Richard went into the classroom first. Some of the kids laughed when they saw him. He smiled. Richard talked to the teacher for a minute. He told her that a bully had drawn the mustache on Sam's face. Then he announced to the class, "Today is mustache day. Come right up and get your own green mustache. Or choose another color. Red. Blue. Anyone?"

"Be sure to use a washable marker," said the teacher.

Several boys came over to Richard. Two boys wanted green mustaches and one wanted a blue one. Sam stood by Richard as he drew each mustache.

"Are you okay now?" asked Richard.

Sam nodded.

Richard walked back to his own classroom. Some of the kids looked surprised when they saw his mustache. Kevin laughed out loud. Richard felt like punching him for making Sam cry, but decided to just ignore him. It was time to talk to Mrs. Steele.

After the rest of the class had left for recess, Richard told Mrs. Steele that he had a problem.

"Does it have something to do with Sam and Daniel?" she asked.

"Well, mostly Sam," said Richard. "The poor kid just came to our school and he doesn't have any friends yet. Kevin calls him a four-eyed nose-wipe and for a while he was stealing his brownies. Then today he drew a green mustache on Sam's face."

"Ah, so that's why you've got a mustache today," said Mrs. Steele.

"Sam stopped crying after I drew a mustache on my face and on Daniel's," said Richard. "I've tried to help Sam, but now I don't know what to do."

"I'm so proud of you for helping Sam. And I'm glad you're telling me about this," said Mrs. Steele. "I'll mention it to his teacher as well. Kevin is being a bully, and we do not tolerate bullies here. Sam needs help, too. If we can help him feel stronger, he won't be a target for such cruel attacks."

"You mean I have to teach Sam to be brave?" asked Richard. "Sam is a scaredy-cat a lot of the time."

"You can show him how to be brave by standing up to Kevin yourself. Tell Kevin you're not going to let him bully Sam anymore," said Mrs. Steele. "I'll back you up. Sometimes boys like Kevin need to learn from other students that their behavior won't be tolerated."

"He might put more crickets in my peanut butter sandwiches," said Richard.

"Has he done that?" Mrs. Steele looked shocked.

"Well, I put two crickets in his brownie," said Richard.

Mrs. Steele still had her mouth open.

"Well, it wasn't really his brownie," Richard went on. "He stole it from Sam."

"And Sam likes cricket brownies?" asked Mrs. Steele.

"No, after I found out that Kevin was stealing Sam's brownies on the way to school, I made a special cricket brownie."

"Ahhh," said Mrs. Steele. "It might be better to confront a bully than to play tricks on him. Kevin obviously didn't get the message."

"I don't know if Kevin will listen to me," said Richard.

"Try it," said Mrs. Steele. "You might be surprised. Sam's teacher can help by sending another student to the bathroom with him. And keep me informed about Sam and Kevin. We won't let this go on."

After school, Sam and Daniel were talking together when Richard entered the classroom.

"I told Daniel all about Ruby," said Sam. "I told him how she stood up, waving her legs and showing her fangs when you tried to pick her up."

"I want to see her do that," said Daniel.

Richard walked them back to his classroom. Sam and Daniel rushed over to Ruby's cage.

"What's she doing?" asked Daniel.

Richard leaned down so that he could see the tarantula. "She's holding a cricket by her mouth so she can eat it."

"Wow," said Daniel. "She's a scary-looking spider, isn't she?"

"Yes, she is," agreed Richard. And that gave him a great idea.

When he got home, he searched through his drawers. He knew he had some vampire fangs somewhere. He'd give them to Sam and tell him they were tarantula fangs. Whenever he wore them, he'd be as brave as Ruby. Maybe Sam should hold Ruby first. That would be a test of his bravery. The more Richard thought about it, the better he felt about it. The only problem was, Richard hadn't held Ruby yet. He hoped she was a calm, easy-going tarantula. Most Chilean rose tarantulas were.

Richard called Sam and told him he'd be at his house early the next day. He had a new plan to defeat Bully-butt.

* * *

Sam was ready when Richard got to his house the next morning. "What's the new plan?"

"I have tarantula fangs for you to wear when you feel scared," said Richard. "They will make you feel brave." He took the fangs out of his pocket.

"They look like Dracula fangs," said Sam.

"Dracula fangs are very similar to tarantula fangs," said Richard. "Fangs are scary no matter whose fangs they are. Nobody likes to mess with a creature with fangs."

Sam didn't look convinced, but he took the fangs. "Should I put them on now?"

"You can wait until we get to school," said Richard. "And there's one more thing you need to do."

"What?" said Sam.

"You need to hold Ruby," said Richard.

Now Sam looked scared. "What if she bites me?"

"I don't think tarantulas bite people very often," said Richard. "I've held lots of tarantulas and I've never been bitten. But I'll make sure Ruby is in a good mood before we try anything. You just have to wear your fangs and act brave."

"Okay," said Sam.

They were so early that no one was in the classroom yet. Mrs. Steele's coat was on her chair, but she was probably in the office or the teachers' lounge. Richard took the tarantula cage and put it on the floor. Ruby had backed into her flowerpot.

"Okay, Sam," said Richard. "Put on your fangs."

Sam put the fangs in his mouth.

"Now act like a fierce tarantula," said Richard.

Sam raised his arms and showed his fangs.

"Yes, wow, you're really fierce!" said Richard.

Sam growled.

Richard smiled as he took the lid off the tarantula's cage. Sam looked cute with fangs. Now for the hard part. Richard took a deep breath, lifted the flowerpot out of the cage, and put it on the floor. Ruby didn't come out of the pot. He shook the pot a little and kind of dumped her out. Would she be mad? Would she run away? No, she just sat there. He put his hand flat on the floor in front of her and touched one of her back legs. She walked slowly onto his hand. Yes!

"Now, put your hand next to my hand," Richard told Sam.

Sam did as he was told. Richard touched Ruby's back leg again and the tarantula walked onto Sam's hand.

"You did it," Richard said. "Now you have Tarantula Power."

Richard got the tarantula to walk onto his hand again, and then he lowered Ruby into her cage. He let out a sigh of relief. Ruby was a calm, well-mannered tarantula. She must have been stressed when he'd tried to pick her up last week.

"We both need to wash our hands now after handling Ruby," Richard told Sam, "in case any of her hairs fell on them. Be careful not to touch your eyes. You could rub tarantula hair into your eyes and that's bad news."

"Hey, what's that nose-wipe doing in our classroom?" Kevin stood in the doorway. "We're not allowed to mess with the tarantula when Mrs. Steele isn't here."

Holding Ruby was the easy part, thought Richard. Now he had to show Sam how to talk back to a bully. Richard took a deep breath. "I'm not going to let you pick on Sam anymore," he said.

Kevin looked surprised. "What did you say to me?"

Richard said it again, louder this time. "I'm not going to let you pick on Sam."

Sam raised his arms, showed his fangs, and growled at Kevin.

Kevin laughed. "Who do you think you are, you little nerd?"

"Tarantula Power!" said Sam. And he growled again.

Kevin shook his head. "Tarantula Power? Is that some kind of new cereal?"

Richard stared at him. Kevin was trying to be a smart aleck, but it was actually a good idea. "I like that," said Richard. "Thanks, Kevin. I'll use that for my cereal project."

"Oh." Kevin sort of smiled. "You're welcome."

"But his name is Sam, not 'little nerd' or 'nose-wipe,'" said Richard.

"Whatever," said Kevin. And he walked back to his desk and sat down.

Chapter 11

That afternoon, Richard left school with both Sam and Daniel. "Where do you live?" Richard asked Daniel.

"I live on Grape Street," he said. "But I'm going to Sam's house today."

"Okay, we'll make a quick left here and head for Sam's," said Richard. "And while we walk, I need you guys to help me with my homework."

"You do?" Sam was wide-eyed.

"Yes, I need a slogan for my new cereal," said Richard.

"For my cereal, you mean?" said Sam.

"Yes, for Tarantula Power," said Richard.

"What's a slogan?" asked Daniel.

"It's just some words that tell you how good the cereal tastes or how good it is for you," explained Richard.

"Helps you fight bullies!" Sam grabbed Richard's hand and grinned.

"And grow strong, too!" Daniel held Richard's other hand.

"That's perfect!" said Richard.

After he dropped the boys off, Richard spent hours working on his new, improved cereal box. Drawing a tarantula was hard. The first time he drew it, he didn't leave enough room around the head for all eight legs plus the pedipalps, the two little legs used for eating. He tried again, but this time he didn't leave room for the fangs. On the third try, he got all the body parts to fit. Richard wrote the name of the cereal in big black letters and used the slogan Sam and Daniel had suggested. It was nearly bedtime when he finished. His cereal project was going to be better than anyone else's. Better than Flower Power. Better than Shark Attack.

The next day, Richard and Jenny waited outside for school to start. They watched Sam and Daniel arrive together. When Kevin walked by them, Sam and Daniel hissed and yelled, "Tarantula Power!" They both wore waxy Halloween fangs.

Kevin stepped back. He started to say something, but then looked around and saw Richard and Jenny watching him. He scowled and walked away.

"You really made Sam brave," said Jenny. "And Daniel, too. Look at those big smiles on their faces."

"Kevin didn't look too happy," said Richard.

"Serves him right," said Jenny.

The morning went by quickly. They had art and P.E. On the way back from art, they passed Sam's classroom. The second graders had just returned from recess and were lined up in the hallway, still wearing their coats. Sam stood at the back of the line with Daniel. As Kevin passed them, Sam and Daniel hissed and shouted, "Tarantula Power!" Many of Sam's classmates hissed, too. Kevin hurried away with his head down.

After lunch, everyone put the finishing touches on their cereal projects. Kevin sat slumped at his desk, playing with a rubber band.

"Are you all finished, Kevin?" Mrs. Steele asked.

Kevin shrugged.

"If your project is finished, you can start your reading homework now." Mrs. Steele took the rubber band.

Kevin got a book out of his desk, but he didn't open it. He rolled a piece of paper into a ball, turned around, and flicked it at Richard.

"What's the matter with you?" Richard glared at Kevin.

"They're always hissing at me," said Kevin. "Thanks to you."

"Sam hisses at you?" said Richard. He couldn't help smiling.

"Yeah, that little punk and all his buddies."

"Good for them," said Jenny. "You were mean to Sam."

"I didn't do anything today," said Kevin.

"You stole his brownies," said Richard.

"I can't give them back," said Kevin. "I ate them. You want me to barf them up?"

"Food only stays in your stomach for one to

three hours," said Susan, leaning over Jenny's desk and looking right at Kevin. "It's too late."

"I'm so glad you told me that." Kevin leaned over and stared right back at her.

"What about making him some brownies?" said Richard.

Kevin snarled, "I don't know how to make brownies."

"Anyone with half a brain can make brownies from a mix," said Susan.

"Sometimes only a quarter of my brain works," said Kevin. "Will I still be able to follow the directions?"

Susan shook her head and went back to her cereal project.

"I think I'll put crickets in my brownies," said Kevin. "That would make them more nutritious."

"If you do that, Sam's whole class will hiss at you," said Jenny.

Kevin rolled his eyes. "Most of them hiss at me already."

When Richard entered the classroom on Monday morning, he saw two insect food items on the board. Today's special entree was "mealworm fried rice," with "cricket brownies" for dessert. Uh-oh.

He wondered if Kevin had made cricket brownies for Sam. He watched as Mrs. Steele came into the room. She looked at the board and smiled.

"Put your cereal boxes on the windowsill," said Mrs. Steele. She pointed to the schedule on the board. "You can share your projects after math and reading groups."

"I want to share my cereal now," said Kevin.

"After math and reading," said Mrs. Steele firmly.

Kevin set his cereal box next to Susan's.

Richard looked at some of the projects. Susan's was especially good. And so was Kevin's Shark Attack. The tarantula picture on Richard's box was not as good as Susan's flowers or Kevin's sharks. He sighed and set his box down.

After reading groups, Susan was the first one to show off her cereal box. She stood in front of the class and explained each different flower she'd used and its shape. Her blouse even had flowers on it.

Richard had to admit she'd done a great job. "Your box is very attractive and colorful," he told her.

Susan looked pleased.

Rana showed her Butterfly Bites next. Richard could tell she had worked with Susan. Her butterflies were sitting on flowers.

"Your box looks great," said Richard.

"Your butterfly facts are very interesting," said Jenny.

When Kevin showed his Shark Attack cereal, some of the boys cheered.

"That's a really unusual cereal idea," said Susan, "and I like the shark pictures."

Kevin smiled and even bowed to the boys who had cheered for the cereal.

Richard felt good about Kevin's success. It surprised him a little, since Kevin had stolen his idea. Of course, it was Richard's idea that everyone was praising. Even so, Kevin had done a good job.

"Richard, why don't you show your project next," said Mrs. Steele.

Richard told the class that he'd given his cereal a new name. It was now called Tarantula Power. He showed the world map on the back of the box and read about some of the countries where people ate insects.

"At first I thought your cereal idea was disgusting," said Susan. "But I didn't know that some people eat insects. I think your project is really educational."

"W-well, thanks," Richard stammered. He had thought his project wasn't as good as Susan's, but maybe he was wrong. Richard squared his shoulders and stood up straighter.

Kevin raised his hand. "I like the bright red color on the front of the box. And all the information about bugs on the back. You always have good ideas, Richard."

Richard stared at Kevin. Maybe this was a new Kevin. Or maybe an alien had taken over Kevin's body. Either way, it was a nice change.

As Richard sat down, he leaned toward Kevin and whispered, "How about beetle burritos?"

Kevin whispered back, "And termite tacos."

The two boys grinned at each other.

After school, Richard stood by the tarantula cage. Ruby had climbed up the side using her sticky feet. "You're an inspiration, Ruby," Richard said softly. "You're small but very brave."

Sam burst into the room. "Look what I made in art class!" Sam held a picture out for Richard to see and pointed to a big red person on the left of the paper. "This is Super Richard."

"You mean I'm the guy wearing the red cape?" asked Richard.

"Yes," said Sam. "Superheroes wear capes."

"Right," said Richard.

Sam pointed to a small person standing next to a big monster. "The monster guy is Mr. Bully-butt. He's wearing a shirt with 'BB' on it."

"He looks very mean and scary," said Richard.

"He used to be mean and scary, but not anymore," said Sam. "Mr. BB is scared of me because of my Tarantula Power! And I'm the little guy in the middle. I'm smiling!"

Richard said, "Wow, Sam, this is great!"

"I made it for you," said Sam. He took his backpack off, unzipped it, and pulled out a plastic bag. "Want a brownie?"

"Sure," said Richard. "Did your mother bake them?"

"Kevin made them for me." Sam took a brownie from the bag.

"Really?" said Richard. "What did he say when he gave them to you?"

"Kevin said he'd give me brownies if I'd stop hissing."

"And what did you say?"

"Daniel was with me," said Sam. "He told Kevin that he's a big bully. And I told Kevin that I'm really mad at him."

"Good job!" said Richard.

Sam grinned. "So Kevin said, 'Sorry, have a brownie.'"

"And then what happened?"

"Daniel and I ate a brownie."

Richard took the bag and looked inside. "Did Kevin put crickets in them?"

"I don't know." Sam looked closely at the brownie in his hand.

Richard bit into a brownie and chewed it slowly. "No crunchy crickets." He took another bite and shook his head. "I'm afraid there aren't even mealworms or termites."

"Let's eat them all anyway," said Sam.

And they did. They ate every last one.